Sarah, Plain and Tall

ALSO BY PATRICIA MacLACHLAN

PATRICIA MacLACHLAN

Sarah, Plain and Tall

A CHARLOTTE ZOLOTOW BOOK

HarperTrophy®
An Imprint of HarperCollinsPublishers

Sarah, Plain and Tall
Copyright © 1985 by Patricia MacLachlan
All rights reserved. No part of this book may be used or reproduced in any manner
whatsoever without written permission except in the case of brief quotations embodied
in critical articles and reviews. Printed in the United States of America. For information
address HarperCollins Children's Books, a division of HarperCollins Publishers,
1350 Avenue of the Americas, New York, NY 10019.

Library of Congress Cataloging-in-Publication Data
MacLachlan, Patricia.
Sarah, plain and tall.
p.   cm.
Summary: When their father invites a mail-order bride to come live with them in their
prairie home, Caleb and Anna are captivated by her and hope that she will stay.
ISBN 0-06-024101-2 — ISBN 0-06-024102-0 (lib. bdg.)
ISBN 0-06-440205-3 (pbk.)
1. Children's stories, American. [1. Stepmothers—Fiction. 2. Frontier and pioneer
life—Fiction.] I. Title.
PZ7.M2225 Sar 1984   83-49481
[Fic]   CIP
                                                                                              AC

First Harper Trophy edition, 1987
Revised Harper Trophy edition, 2004
❖
Visit us on the World Wide Web!
www.harperchildrens.com

For old friends, dear friends—
DICK AND WENDY PUFF,
ALLISON AND DEREK

Sarah, Plain and Tall

1

"Did Mama sing every day?" asked Caleb. "Every-single-day?" He sat close to the fire, his chin in his hand. It was dusk, and the dogs lay beside him on the warm hearth-stones.

"Every-single-day," I told him for the second time this week. For the twentieth time this month. The hundredth time this year? And the past few years?

"And did Papa sing, too?"

"Yes. Papa sang, too. Don't get so close, Caleb. You'll heat up."

He pushed his chair back. It made a hollow scraping sound on the hearthstones, and the dogs stirred. Lottie, small and black, wagged her tail and lifted her head. Nick slept on.

I turned the bread dough over and over on the marble slab on the kitchen table.

"Well, Papa doesn't sing anymore," said Caleb very softly. A log broke apart and crackled in the fireplace. He looked up at me. "What did I look like when I was born?"

"You didn't have any clothes on," I told him.

"I know that," he said.

"You looked like this." I held the bread dough up in a round pale ball.

"I had hair," said Caleb seriously.

"Not enough to talk about," I said.

"And she named me Caleb," he went on, filling in the old familiar story.

"*I* would have named you Troublesome," I

said, making Caleb smile.

"And Mama handed me to you in the yellow blanket and said . . ." He waited for me to finish the story. "And said . . . ?"

I sighed. "And Mama said, 'Isn't he beautiful, Anna?'"

"And I was," Caleb finished.

Caleb thought the story was over, and I didn't tell him what I had really thought. He was homely and plain, and he had a terrible holler and a horrid smell. But these were not the worst of him. Mama died the next morning. That was the worst thing about Caleb.

"Isn't he beautiful, Anna?" Her last words to me. I had gone to bed thinking how wretched he looked. And I forgot to say good night.

I wiped my hands on my apron and went to the window. Outside, the prairie reached out and touched the places where the sky came down. Though winter was nearly over,

there were patches of snow and ice everywhere. I looked at the long dirt road that
crawled across the plains, remembering the
morning that Mama had died, cruel and
sunny. They had come for her in a wagon and
taken her away to be buried. And then the
cousins and aunts and uncles had come and
tried to fill up the house. But they couldn't.

Slowly, one by one, they left. And then
the days seemed long and dark like winter
days, even though it wasn't winter. And Papa
didn't sing.

Isn't he beautiful, Anna?

No, Mama.

It was hard to think of Caleb as beautiful.
It took three whole days for me to love him,
sitting in the chair by the fire, Papa washing
up the supper dishes, Caleb's tiny hand
brushing my cheek. And a smile. It was the
smile, I know.

"Can you remember her songs?" asked

Caleb. "Mama's songs?"

I turned from the window. "No. Only that she sang about flowers and birds. Sometimes about the moon at nighttime."

Caleb reached down and touched Lottie's head.

"Maybe," he said, his voice low, "if you remember the songs, then I might remember her, too."

My eyes widened and tears came. Then the door opened and wind blew in with Papa, and I went to stir the stew. Papa put his arms around me and put his nose in my hair.

"Nice soapy smell, that stew," he said.

I laughed. "That's my hair."

Caleb came over and threw his arms around Papa's neck and hung down as Papa swung him back and forth, and the dogs sat up.

"Cold in town," said Papa. "And Jack was feisty." Jack was Papa's horse that he'd raised from a colt. "Rascal," murmured Papa, smiling, because no matter what Jack did Papa loved him.

I spooned up the stew and lighted the oil lamp and we ate with the dogs crowding under the table, hoping for spills or handouts.

Papa might not have told us about Sarah that night if Caleb hadn't asked him the question. After the dishes were cleared and washed and Papa was filling the tin pail with ashes, Caleb spoke up. It wasn't a question, really.

"You don't sing anymore," he said. He said it harshly. Not because he meant to, but because he had been thinking of it for so long. "Why?" he asked more gently.

Slowly Papa straightened up. There was a long silence, and the dogs looked up, wondering at it.

"I've forgotten the old songs," said Papa quietly. He sat down. "But maybe there's a way to remember them." He looked up at us.

"How?" asked Caleb eagerly.

Papa leaned back in the chair. "I've placed an advertisement in the newspapers. For help."

"You mean a housekeeper?" I asked, surprised.

Caleb and I looked at each other and burst out laughing, remembering Hilly, our old housekeeper. She was round and slow and shuffling. She snored in a high whistle at night, like a teakettle, and let the fire go out.

"No," said Papa slowly. "Not a housekeeper." He paused. "A wife."

Caleb stared at Papa. "A wife? You mean a mother?"

Nick slid his face onto Papa's lap and Papa stroked his ears.

"That, too," said Papa. "Like Maggie."

Matthew, our neighbor to the south, had written to ask for a wife and mother for his children. And Maggie had come from Tennessee. Her hair was the color of turnips and she laughed.

Papa reached into his pocket and unfolded a letter written on white paper. "And I have received an answer." Papa read to us:

"Dear Mr. Jacob Witting,

"I am Sarah Wheaton from Maine as you will see from my letter. I am answering your advertisement. I have never been married, though I have been asked. I have lived with an older brother, William, who is about to be married. His wife-to-be is young and energetic.

"I have always loved to live by the sea, but at this time I feel a move is necessary. And the truth is, the sea is as far east as I can go. My choice, as you can see, is limited. This should not be taken as an insult. I am strong and I work hard and I am willing to travel. But I am not mild mannered. If you should still care to write, I would be interested in your children and about where you live. And you.

   "Very truly yours,

    "Sarah Elisabeth Wheaton

"P.S. Do you have opinions on cats? I have one."

No one spoke when Papa finished the letter. He kept looking at it in his hands, reading it over to himself. Finally I turned my head a bit to sneak a look at Caleb. He was smiling. I smiled too.

"One thing," I said in the quiet of the room.

"What's that?" asked Papa, looking up.

I put my arm around Caleb.

"Ask her if she sings," I said.

2

Caleb and Papa and I wrote letters to Sarah, and before the ice and snow had melted from the fields, we all received answers. Mine came first.

Dear Anna,

Yes, I can braid hair and I can make stew and bake bread, though I prefer to build bookshelves and paint.

My favorite colors are the colors of the sea, blue and gray and green, depending on the weather. My brother William is a fisherman, and he tells me that when he is in the middle of a fog-bound sea the water is a color for which there is no name. He catches flounder and sea bass and bluefish. Sometimes he sees whales. And birds, too, of course. I am enclosing a book of sea birds so you will see what William and I see every day.

Very truly yours,
Sarah Elisabeth Wheaton

Caleb read and read the letter so many times that the ink began to run and the folds tore. He read the book about sea birds over and over.

"Do you think she'll come?" asked Caleb. "And will she stay? What if she thinks we are loud and pesky?"

"You *are* loud and pesky," I told him. But I

was worried, too. Sarah loved the sea, I could tell. Maybe she wouldn't leave there after all to come where there were fields and grass and sky and not much else.

"What if she comes and doesn't like our house?" Caleb asked. "I told her it was small. Maybe I shouldn't have told her it was small."

"Hush, Caleb. Hush."

Caleb's letter came soon after, with a picture of a cat drawn on the envelope.

Dear Caleb,

My cat's name is Seal because she is gray like the seals that swim offshore in Maine. She is glad that Lottie and Nick send their greetings. She likes dogs most of the time. She says their footprints are much larger than hers (which she is enclosing in return).

Your house sounds lovely, even though it is far out in the country with no close neighbors. My house is tall and the shingles are gray because of the salt from the sea. There are roses nearby.

Yes, I do like small rooms sometimes. Yes, I can keep a fire going at night. I do not know if I snore. Seal has never told me.

Very truly yours,

Sarah Elisabeth

"Did you really ask her about fires and snoring?" I asked, amazed.

"I wished to know," Caleb said.

He kept the letter with him, reading it in the barn and in the fields and by the cow pond. And always in bed at night.

One morning, early, Papa and Caleb and I were cleaning out the horse stalls and putting down new bedding. Papa stopped suddenly and leaned on his pitchfork.

"Sarah has said she will come for a month's time if we wish her to," he said, his voice loud in the dark barn. "To see how it is. Just to see."

Caleb stood by the stall door and folded his arms across his chest.

"I think," he began. Then, "I think," he said slowly, "that it would be good—to say yes," he finished in a rush.

Papa looked at me.

"I say yes," I told him, grinning.

"Yes," said Papa. "Then yes it is."

And the three of us, all smiling, went to work again.

The next day Papa went to town to mail his letter to Sarah. It was rainy for days, and the clouds followed. The house was cool and damp and quiet. Once I set four places at the table, then caught myself and put the extra plate away. Three lambs were born, one with a black face. And then Papa's letter came. It was very short.

Dear Jacob,

I will come by train. I will wear a yellow
bonnet. I am plain and tall.

Sarah

"What's that?" asked Caleb excitedly,
peering over Papa's shoulder. He pointed.
"There, written at the bottom of the letter."

Papa read it to himself. Then he smiled,
holding up the letter for us to see.

Tell them I sing was all it said.

3

Sarah came in the spring. She came through green grass fields that bloomed with Indian paintbrush, red and orange, and blue-eyed grass.

Papa got up early for the long day's trip to the train and back. He brushed his hair so slick and shiny that Caleb laughed. He wore a clean blue shirt, and a belt instead of suspenders.

He fed and watered the horses, talking to them as he hitched them up to the wagon. Old Bess, calm and kind; Jack, wild-eyed, reaching over to nip Bess on the neck.

"Clear day, Bess," said Papa, rubbing her nose.

"Settle down, Jack." He leaned his head on Jack.

And then Papa drove off along the dirt road to fetch Sarah. Papa's new wife. Maybe. Maybe our new mother.

Gophers ran back and forth across the road, stopping to stand up and watch the wagon. Far off in a field a woodchuck ate and listened. Ate and listened.

Caleb and I did our chores without talking. We shoveled out the stalls and laid down new hay. We fed the sheep. We swept and straightened and carried wood and water. And then our chores were done.

Caleb pulled on my shirt.

"Is my face clean?" he asked. "Can my face be *too* clean?" He looked alarmed.

"No, your face is clean but not too clean," I said.

Caleb slipped his hand into mine as we stood on the porch, watching the road. He was afraid.

"Will she be nice?" he asked. "Like Maggie?"

"Sarah will be nice," I told him.

"How far away is Maine?" he asked.

"You know how far. Far away, by the sea."

"Will Sarah bring some sea?" he asked.

"No, you cannot bring the sea."

The sheep ran in the field, and far off the cows moved slowly to the pond, like turtles.

"Will she like us?" asked Caleb very softly.

I watched a marsh hawk wheel down behind the barn.

He looked up at me.

"Of course she will like us." He answered his own question. "We are nice," he added, making me smile.

We waited and watched. I rocked on the porch and Caleb rolled a marble on the wood floor. Back and forth. Back and forth. The marble was blue.

We saw the dust from the wagon first, rising above the road, above the heads of Jack and Old Bess. Caleb climbed up onto the porch roof and shaded his eyes.

"A bonnet!" he cried. "I see a yellow bonnet!"

The dogs came out from under the porch, ears up, their eyes on the cloud of dust bringing Sarah. The wagon passed the fenced field, and the cows and sheep looked up, too. It rounded the windmill and the barn and the windbreak of Russian olive that Mama had planted long ago. Nick began to bark, then Lottie, and the wagon clattered into the yard and stopped by the steps.

"Hush," said Papa to the dogs.

And it was quiet.

Sarah stepped down from the wagon, a cloth bag in her hand. She reached up and took off her yellow bonnet, smoothing back her brown hair into a bun. She was plain and tall.

"Did you bring some sea?" cried Caleb beside me.

"Something from the sea," said Sarah, smiling. "And me." She turned and lifted a black case from the wagon. "And Seal, too."

Carefully she opened the case, and Seal, gray with white feet, stepped out. Lottie lay down, her head on her paws, staring. Nick leaned down to sniff. Then he lay down, too.

"The cat will be good in the barn," said Papa. "For mice."

Sarah smiled. "She will be good in the house, too."

Sarah took Caleb's hand, then mine. Her hands were large and rough. She gave Caleb a shell—a moon snail, she called it—that was curled and smelled of salt.

"The gulls fly high and drop the shells on the rocks below," she told Caleb. "When the shell is broken, they eat what is inside."

"That is very smart," said Caleb.

"For you, Anna," said Sarah, "a sea stone."

And she gave me the smoothest and whitest stone I had ever seen.

"The sea washes over and over and around the stone, rolling it until it is round and perfect."

"That is very smart, too," said Caleb. He looked up at Sarah. "We do not have the sea here."

Sarah turned and looked out over the plains.

"No," she said. "There is no sea here. But the land rolls a little like the sea."

My father did not see her look, but I did. And I knew that Caleb had seen it, too. Sarah was not smiling. Sarah was already lonely. In a month's time the preacher might come to marry Sarah and Papa. And a month was a long time. Time enough for her to change her mind and leave us.

Papa took Sarah's bags inside, where her room was ready with a quilt on the bed and blue flax dried in a vase on the night table.

Seal stretched and made a small cat sound. I watched her circle the dogs and sniff the air. Caleb came out and stood beside me.

"When will we sing?" he whispered.

I shook my head, turning the white stone over and over in my hand. I wished everything was as perfect as the stone. I wished that Papa and Caleb and I were perfect for Sarah. I wished we had a sea of our own.

4

The dogs loved Sarah first. Lottie slept beside her bed, curled in a soft circle, and Nick leaned his face on the covers in the morning, watching for the first sign that Sarah was awake. No one knew where Seal slept. Seal was a roamer.

Sarah's collection of shells sat on the windowsill.

"A scallop," she told us, picking up the shells one by one, "a sea clam, an oyster, a razor clam. And a conch shell. If you put it to your ear you can hear the sea." She put it to

Caleb's ear, then mine. Papa listened, too.
Then Sarah listened once more, with a look so
sad and far away that Caleb leaned against me.

"At least Sarah can hear the sea," he whispered.

Papa was quiet and shy with Sarah, and so
was I. But Caleb talked to Sarah from morning until the light left the sky.

"Where are you going?" he asked. "To do
what?"

"To pick flowers," said Sarah. "I'll hang
some of them upside down and dry them so
they'll keep some color. And we can have
flowers all winter long."

"I'll come, too!" cried Caleb. "Sarah said
winter," he said to me. "That means Sarah
will stay."

Together we picked flowers, paintbrush
and clover and prairie violets. There were
buds on the wild roses that climbed up the
paddock fence.

"The roses will bloom in early summer," I told Sarah. I looked to see if she knew what I was thinking. Summer was when the wedding would be. *Might* be. Sarah and Papa's wedding.

We hung the flowers from the ceiling in little bunches. "I've never seen this before," said Sarah. "What is it called?"

"Bride's bonnet," I told her.

Caleb smiled at the name.

"We don't have this by the sea," she said. "We have seaside goldenrod and wild asters and woolly ragwort."

"Woolly ragwort!" Caleb whooped. He made up a song.

> *"Woolly ragwort all around,*
> *Woolly ragwort on the ground,*
> *Woolly ragwort grows and grows,*
> *Woolly ragwort in your nose."*

Sarah and Papa laughed, and the dogs lifted their heads and thumped their tails against the wood floor. Seal sat on a kitchen chair and watched us with yellow eyes.

We ate Sarah's stew, the late light coming through the windows. Papa had baked bread that was still warm from the fire.

"The stew is fine," said Papa.

"Ayuh." Sarah nodded. "The bread, too."

"What does 'ayuh' mean?" asked Caleb.

"In Maine it means yes," said Sarah. "Do you want more stew?"

"Ayuh," said Caleb.

"Ayuh," echoed my father.

After dinner Sarah told us about William. "He has a gray-and-white boat named *Kittiwake*." She looked out the window. "That is a small gull found way off the shore where William fishes. There are three aunts who live near us. They wear silk dresses and no shoes. You would love them."

"Ayuh," said Caleb.

"Does your brother look like you?" I asked.

"Yes," said Sarah. "He is plain and tall."

At dusk Sarah cut Caleb's hair on the front steps, gathering his curls and scattering them on the fence and ground. Seal batted some hair around the porch as the dogs watched.

"Why?" asked Caleb.

"For the birds," said Sarah. "They will use it for their nests. Later we can look for nests of curls."

"Sarah said 'later,'" Caleb whispered to me as we spread his hair about. "Sarah will stay."

Sarah cut Papa's hair, too. No one else saw, but I found him behind the barn, tossing the pieces of hair into the wind for the birds.

Sarah brushed my hair and tied it up in back with a rose velvet ribbon she had brought from Maine. She brushed hers long and free and tied it back, too, and we stood side by side looking into the mirror. I looked taller, like Sarah, and fair and thin. And with my hair pulled back I looked a little like her daughter. Sarah's daughter.

And then it was time for singing.

Sarah sang us a song we had never heard before as we sat on the porch, insects buzzing in the dark, the rustle of cows in the grasses. It was called "Sumer Is Icumen in," and she taught it to us all, even Papa, who sang as if he had never stopped singing.

"Sumer is icumen in,
Lhude sing cuccu!"

"What is sumer?" asked Caleb. He said it "soomer," the way Sarah had said it.

"Summer," said Papa and Sarah at the same time. Caleb and I looked at each other. Summer was coming.

"Tomorrow," said Sarah, "I want to see the

sheep. You know, I've never touched one."

"Never?" Caleb sat up.

"Never," said Sarah. She smiled and leaned back in her chair. "But I've touched seals. Real seals. They are cool and slippery and they slide through the water like fish. They can cry and sing. And sometimes they bark, a little like dogs."

Sarah barked like a seal. And Lottie and Nick came running from the barn to jump up on Sarah and lick her face and make her laugh. Sarah stroked them and scratched their ears and it was quiet again.

"I wish I could touch a seal right now," said Caleb, his voice soft in the night.

"So do I," said Sarah. She sighed, then she began to sing the summer song again. Far off in a field, a meadowlark sang, too.

5

The sheep made Sarah smile. She sank her fingers into their thick, coarse wool. She talked to them, running with the lambs, letting them suck on her fingers. She named them after her favorite aunts, Harriet and Mattie and Lou. She lay down in the field beside them and sang "Sumer Is Icumen in," her voice drifting over the meadow grasses, carried by the wind.

She cried when we found a lamb that had died, and she shouted and shook her fist at the turkey buzzards that came from nowhere to eat it. She would not let Caleb or me come near. And that night, Papa went with a shovel to bury the sheep and a lantern to bring Sarah back. She sat on the porch alone. Nick crept up to lean against her knees.

After dinner, Sarah drew pictures to send home to Maine. She began a charcoal drawing of the fields, rolling like the sea rolled. She drew a sheep whose ears were too big. And she drew a windmill.

"Windmill was my first word," said Caleb. "Papa told me so."

"Mine was flower," I said. "What was yours, Sarah?"

"Dune," said Sarah.

"Dune?" Caleb looked up.

"In Maine," said Sarah, "there are rock cliffs that rise up at the edge of the sea. And there are hills covered with pine and spruce trees, green with needles. But William and I found a sand dune all our own. It was soft and sparkling with bits of mica, and when we were little we would slide down the dune into the water."

Caleb looked out the window.

"We have no dunes here," he said.

Papa stood up.

"Yes we do," he said. He took the lantern and went out the door to the barn.

"We do?" Caleb called after him.

He ran ahead, Sarah and I following, the dogs close behind.

Next to the barn was Papa's mound of hay for bedding, nearly as tall as the barn, covered with canvas to keep the rain from rotting it. Papa carried the wooden ladder from the barn and leaned it against the hay.

"There." He smiled at Sarah. "Our dune."

Sarah was very quiet. The dogs looked up at her, waiting. Seal brushed against her legs, her tail in the air. Caleb reached over and took her hand.

"It looks high up," he said. "Are you scared, Sarah?"

"Scared? Scared!" exclaimed Sarah. "You bet I'm not scared."

She climbed the ladder, and Nick began to bark. She climbed to the very top of the hay and sat, looking down at us. Above, the stars were coming out. Papa piled a bed of loose hay below with his pitchfork. The light of the lantern made his eyes shine when he smiled up at Sarah.

"Fine?" called Papa.

"Fine," said Sarah. She lifted her arms over her head and slid down, down, into the soft hay. She lay, laughing, as the dogs rolled beside her.

"Was it a good dune?" called Caleb.

"Yes," said Sarah. "It is a fine dune."

Caleb and I climbed up and slid down. And Sarah did it three more times. At last Papa slid down, too, as the sky grew darker and the stars blinked like fireflies. We were covered with hay and dust, and we sneezed.

In the kitchen, Caleb and I washed in the big wooden tub and Sarah drew more pictures to send to William. One was of Papa, his hair curly and full of hay. She drew Caleb, sliding down the hay, his arms like Sarah's over his head. And she drew a picture of me in the tub, my hair long and straight and wet. She looked at her drawing of the fields for a long time.

"Something is missing," she told Caleb. "Something." And she put it away.

"'Dear William,'" Sarah read to us by lantern light that night. "'Sliding down our dune of hay is almost as fine as sliding down the sand dunes into the sea.'"

Caleb smiled at me across the table. He said nothing, but his mouth formed the words I had heard, too. *Our dune.*

6

The days grew longer. The cows moved close to the pond, where the water was cool and there were trees.

Papa taught Sarah how to plow the fields, guiding the plow behind Jack and Old Bess, the reins around her neck. When the chores were done we sat in the meadow with the sheep, Sarah beside us, watching Papa finish.

"Tell me about winter," said Sarah.

Old Bess nodded her head as she walked, but we could hear Papa speak sharply to Jack.

"Jack doesn't like work," said Caleb. "He

wants to be here in the sweet grass with us."

"I don't blame him," said Sarah. She lay back in the grass with her arms under her head. "Tell me about winter," she said again.

"Winter is cold here," said Caleb, and Sarah and I laughed.

"Winter is cold everywhere," I said.

"We go to school in winter," said Caleb. "Sums and writing and books," he sang.

"I am good at sums and writing," said Sarah. "I love books. How do you get to school?"

"Papa drives us in the wagon. Or we walk the three miles when there is not too much snow."

Sarah sat up. "Do you have lots of snow?"

"Lots and lots and lots of snow," chanted Caleb, rolling around in the grass. "Sometimes we have to dig our way out to feed the animals."

"In Maine the barns are attached to the

houses sometimes," said Sarah.

Caleb grinned. "So you could have a cow to Sunday supper?"

Sarah and I laughed.

"When there are bad storms, Papa ties a rope from the house to the barn so no one will get lost," said Caleb.

I frowned. I loved winter.

"There is ice on the windows on winter mornings," I told Sarah. "We can draw sparkling pictures and we can see our breath in the air. Papa builds a warm fire, and we bake hot biscuits and put on hundreds of sweaters. And if the snow is too high, we stay home from school and make snow people."

Sarah lay back in the tall grasses again, her face nearly hidden.

"And is there wind?" she asked.

"Do you like wind?" asked Caleb.

"There is wind by the sea," said Sarah.

"There is wind here," said Caleb happily.

"It blows the snow and brings tumbleweeds and makes the sheep run. Wind and wind and wind!" Caleb stood up and ran like the wind, and the sheep ran after him. Sarah and I watched him jump over rocks and gullies, the sheep behind him, stiff legged and fast. He circled the field, the sun making the top of his hair golden. He collapsed next to Sarah, and the lambs pushed their wet noses into us.

"Hello, Lou," said Sarah, smiling. "Hello, Mattie."

The sun rose higher, and Papa stopped to take off his hat and wipe his face with his sleeve.

"I'm hot," said Sarah. "I can't wait for winter wind. Let's swim."

"Swim where?" I asked her.

"I can't swim," said Caleb.

"Can't swim!" exclaimed Sarah. "I'll teach you in the cow pond."

"That's for cows!" I cried.

But Sarah had grabbed our hands and we were running through the fields, ducking under the fence to the far pond.

"Shoo, cows," said Sarah as the cows looked up, startled. She took off her dress and waded into the water in her petticoat. She dived suddenly and disappeared for a moment as Caleb and I watched. She came up, laughing, her hair streaming free. Water beads sat on her shoulders.

She tried to teach us how to float. I sank like a bucket filled with water and came up sputtering. But Caleb lay on his back and learned how to blow streams of water high in the air like a whale. The cows stood on the banks of the pond and stared and stopped their chewing. Water bugs circled us.

"Is this like the sea?" asked Caleb.

Sarah treaded water.

"The sea is salt," said Sarah. "It stretches out as far as you can see. It gleams like the sun on glass. There are waves."

"Like this?" asked Caleb, and he pushed a wave at Sarah, making her cough and laugh.

"Yes," she said. "Like that."

I held my breath and floated at last, looking up into the sky, afraid to speak. Crows flew over, three in a row. And I could hear a killdeer in the field.

We climbed the bank and dried ourselves and lay in the grass again. The cows watched, their eyes sad in their dinner-plate faces. And I slept, dreaming a perfect dream. The fields had turned to a sea that gleamed like sun on glass. And Sarah was happy.

7

The dandelions in the fields had gone by, their heads soft as feathers. The summer roses were opening.

Our neighbors, Matthew and Maggie, came to help Papa plow up a new field for corn. Sarah stood with us on the porch, watching their wagon wind up the road, two horses pulling it and one tied in back. I remembered the last time we had stood here alone, Caleb and I, waiting for Sarah.

Sarah's hair was in thick braids that circled her head, wild daisies tucked here and there. Papa had picked them for her.

Old Bess and Jack ran along the inside of the fence, whickering at the new horses.

"Papa needs five horses for the big gang plow," Caleb told Sarah. "Prairie grass is hard."

Matthew and Maggie came with their two children and a sackful of chickens. Maggie emptied the sack into the yard and three red banty chickens clucked and scattered.

"They are for you," she told Sarah. "For eating."

Sarah loved the chickens. She clucked back to them and fed them grain. They followed her, shuffling and scratching primly in the dirt. I knew they would not be for eating.

The children were young and named Rose and Violet, after flowers. They hooted and laughed and chased the chickens, who flew up to the porch roof, then the dogs, who crept quietly under the porch. Seal had long ago fled to the barn to sleep in cool hay.

Sarah and Maggie helped hitch the horses to the plow, then they set up a big table in the shade of the barn, covering it with a quilt and a kettle of flowers in the middle. They sat on the porch while Caleb and Matthew and Papa began their morning of plowing. I mixed biscuit dough just inside the door, watching.

"You are lonely, yes?" asked Maggie in her soft voice.

Sarah's eyes filled with tears. Slowly I stirred the dough.

Maggie reached over and took Sarah's hand.

"I miss the hills of Tennessee sometimes," she said.

Do not miss the hills, Maggie, I thought.

"I miss the sea," said Sarah.

Do not miss the hills. Do not miss the sea.

I stirred and stirred the dough.

"I miss my brother William," said Sarah. "But he is married. The house is hers now. Not mine any longer. There are three old aunts who all squawk together like crows at dawn. I miss them, too."

"There are always things to miss," said Maggie. "No matter where you are."

I looked out and saw Papa and Matthew and Caleb working. Rose and Violet ran in the fields. I felt something brush my legs and looked down at Nick, wagging his tail.

"I would miss you, Nick," I whispered. "I would." I knelt down and scratched his ears. "I miss Mama."

"I nearly forgot," said Maggie on the porch. "I have something more for you."

I carried the bowl outside and watched Maggie lift a low wooden box out of the wagon.

"Plants," she said to Sarah. "For your garden."

"My garden?" Sarah bent down to touch the plants.

"Zinnias and marigolds and wild fever-few," said Maggie. "You must have a garden. Wherever you are."

Sarah smiled. "I had a garden in Maine with dahlias and columbine. And nasturtiums the color of the sun when it sets. I don't know if nasturtiums would grow here."

"Try," said Maggie. "You must have a garden."

We planted the flowers by the porch, turning over the soil and patting it around them, and watering. Lottie and Nick came to sniff, and the chickens walked in the dirt, leaving prints. In the fields, the horses pulled the plow up and down under the hot summer sun.

Maggie wiped her face, leaving a streak of dirt.

"Soon you can drive your wagon over to

my house and I will give you more. I have tansy."

Sarah frowned. "I have never driven a wagon."

"I can teach you," said Maggie. "And so can Anna and Caleb. And Jacob."

Sarah turned to me.

"Can you?" she asked. "Can you drive a wagon?"

I nodded.

"And Caleb?"

"Yes."

"In Maine," said Sarah, "I would walk to town."

"Here it is different," said Maggie. "Here you will drive."

Way off in the sky, clouds gathered. Matthew and Papa and Caleb came in from the fields, their work done. We all ate in the shade.

"We are glad you are here," said Matthew

to Sarah. "A new friend. Maggie misses her friends sometimes."

Sarah nodded. "There is always something to miss, no matter where you are," she said, smiling at Maggie.

Rose and Violet fell asleep in the grass, their bellies full of meat and greens and biscuits. And when it was time to go, Papa and Matthew lifted them into the wagon to sleep on blankets.

Sarah walked slowly behind the wagon for a long time, waving, watching it disappear. Caleb and I ran to bring her back, the chickens running wildly behind us.

"What shall we name them?" asked Sarah, laughing as the chickens followed us into the house.

I smiled. I was right. The chickens would not be for eating.

And then Papa came, just before the rain, bringing Sarah the first roses of summer.

8

The rain came and passed, but strange clouds hung in the northwest, low and black and green. And the air grew still.

In the morning, Sarah dressed in a pair of overalls and went to the barn to have an argument with Papa. She took apples for Old Bess and Jack.

"Women don't wear overalls," said Caleb, running along behind her like one of Sarah's chickens.

"This woman does," said Sarah crisply.

Papa stood by the fence.

"I want to learn how to ride a horse," Sarah told him. "And then I want to learn how to drive the wagon. By myself."

Jack leaned over and nipped at Sarah's overalls. She fed him an apple. Caleb and I stood behind Sarah.

"I can ride a horse, I know," said Sarah. "I rode once when I was twelve. I will ride Jack." Jack was Sarah's favorite.

Papa shook his head. "Not Jack," he said. "Jack is sly."

"I am sly, too," said Sarah stubbornly.

Papa smiled. "Ayuh," he said, nodding. "But not Jack."

"Yes, Jack!" Sarah's voice was very loud.

"I can teach you how to drive a wagon. I have already taught you how to plow."

"And then I can go to town. By myself."

"Say no, Papa," Caleb whispered beside me.

"That's a fair thing, Sarah," said Papa. "We'll practice."

A soft rumble of thunder sounded. Papa looked up at the clouds.

"Today?" Can we begin today?" asked Sarah.

"Tomorrow is best," said Papa, looking worried. "I have to fix the house roof. A portion of it is loose. And there's a storm coming."

"We," said Sarah.

"What?" Papa turned.

"*We* will fix the roof," said Sarah. "I've done it before. I know about roofs. I am a good carpenter. Remember, I told you?"

There was thunder again, and Papa went to get the ladder.

"Are you fast?" he asked Sarah.

"I am fast and I am good," said Sarah. And they climbed the ladder to the roof, Sarah with wisps of hair around her face, her mouth full of nails, overalls like Papa's. Overalls that *were* Papa's.

Caleb and I went inside to close the

windows. We could hear the steady sound of hammers pounding the roof overhead.

"Why does she want to go to town by herself?" asked Caleb. "To leave us?"

I shook my head, weary with Caleb's questions. Tears gathered at the corners of my eyes. But there was no time to cry, for suddenly Papa called out.

"Caleb! Anna!"

We ran outside and saw a huge cloud, horribly black, moving toward us over the north fields. Papa slid down the roof, helping Sarah after him.

"A squall!" he yelled to us. He held up his arms and Sarah jumped off the porch roof.

"Get the horses inside," he ordered Caleb. "Get the sheep, Anna. And the cows. The barn is safest."

The grasses flattened. There was a hiss of wind, a sudden pungent smell. Our faces looked yellow in the strange light. Caleb and

I jumped over the fence and found the animals huddled by the barn. I counted the sheep to make sure they were all there, and herded them into a large stall. A few raindrops came, gentle at first, then stronger and louder, so that Caleb and I covered our ears and stared at each other without speaking. Caleb looked frightened and I tried to smile at him. Sarah carried a sack into the barn, her hair wet and streaming down her neck, Papa came behind, Lottie and Nick with him, their ears flat against their heads.

"Wait!" cried Sarah. "My chickens!"

"No, Sarah!" Papa called after her. But Sarah had already run from the barn into a sheet of rain. My father followed her. The sheep nosed open their stall door and milled around the barn, bleating. Nick crept under my arm, and a lamb, Mattie with the black face, stood close to me, trembling. There was a soft paw on my lap, then a gray body. Seal.

And then, as the thunder pounded and the wind rose and there was the terrible crackling of lightning close by, Sarah and Papa stood in the barn doorway, wet to the skin. Papa carried Sarah's chickens. Sarah came with an armful of summer roses.

Sarah's chickens were not afraid, and they settled like small red bundles in the hay. Papa closed the door at last, shutting out some of the sounds of the storm. The barn was eerie and half lighted, like dusk without a lantern. Papa spread blankets around our shoulders and Sarah unpacked a bag of cheese and bread and jam. At the very bottom of the bag were Sarah's shells.

Caleb got up and went over to the small barn window.

"What color is the sea when it storms?" he asked Sarah.

"Blue," said Sarah, brushing her wet hair back with her fingers. "And gray and green."

Caleb nodded and smiled.

"Look," he said to her. "Look what is missing from your drawing."

Sarah went to stand between Caleb and Papa by the window. She looked a long time without speaking. Finally, she touched Papa's shoulder.

"We have squalls in Maine, too," she said. "Just like this. It will be all right, Jacob."

Papa said nothing. But he put his arm around her, and leaned over to rest his chin in her hair. I closed my eyes, suddenly remembering Mama and Papa standing that way, Mama smaller than Sarah, her hair fair against Papa's shoulder. When I opened my eyes again, it was Sarah standing there. Caleb looked at me and smiled and smiled until he could smile no more.

We slept in the hay all night, waking when the wind was wild, sleeping again when it was quiet. And at dawn there was the sudden sound of hail, like stones tossed against the barn. We stared out the window, watching the ice marbles bounce on the ground. And when it was over we opened the barn door and walked out into the early-morning light. The hail crunched and melted beneath our feet. It was white and gleaming for as far as we looked, like sun on glass. Like the sea.

9

It was very quiet. The dogs leaned down to eat the hailstones. Seal stepped around them and leaped up on the fence to groom herself. A tree had blown over near the cow pond. And the wild roses were scattered on the ground, as if a wedding had come and gone there. "I'm glad I saved an armful" was all that Sarah said.

Only one field was badly damaged, and Sarah and Papa hitched up the horses and plowed and replanted during the next two days. The roof had held.

"I told you I know about roofs," Sarah told Papa, making him smile.

Papa kept his promise to Sarah. When the work was done, he took her out into the fields, Papa riding Jack who was sly, and Sarah riding Old Bess. Sarah was quick to learn.

"Too quick," Caleb complained to me as we watched from the fence. He thought a moment. "Maybe she'll fall off and have to stay here. Why?" he asked, turning to me. "Why does she have to go away alone?"

"Hush up, Caleb," I said crossly. "Hush up."

"I could get sick and make her stay here," said Caleb.

"No."

"We could tie her up."

"No."

And Caleb began to cry, and I took him inside the barn where we could both cry.

Papa and Sarah came to hitch the horses

to the wagon, so Sarah could practice driving. Papa didn't see Caleb's tears, and he sent him with an ax to begin chopping up the tree by the pond for firewood. I stood and watched Sarah, the reins in her hands, Papa next to her in the wagon. I could see Caleb standing by the pond, one hand shading his eyes, watching, too. I went into the safe darkness of the barn then, Sarah's chickens scuttling along behind me.

"Why?" I asked out loud, echoing Caleb's question.

The chickens watched me, their eyes small and bright.

The next morning Sarah got up early and put on her blue dress. She took apples to the barn. She loaded a bundle of hay on the wagon for Old Bess and Jack. She put on her yellow bonnet.

"Remember Jack," said Papa. "A strong hand."

"Yes, Jacob."

"Best to be home before dark," said Papa. "Driving a wagon is hard if there's no full moon."

"Yes, Jacob."

Sarah kissed us all, even my father, who looked surprised.

"Take care of Seal," she said to Caleb and me. And with a whisper to Old Bess and a stern word to Jack, Sarah climbed up in the wagon and drove away.

"Very good," murmured Papa as he watched. And after a while he turned and went out into the fields.

Caleb and I watched Sarah from the porch. Caleb took my hand, and the dogs lay down beside us. It was sunny, and I remembered another time when a wagon had taken Mama away. It had been a day just like this day. And Mama had never come back.

Seal jumped up to the porch, her feet

making a small thump. Caleb leaned down and picked her up and walked inside. I took the broom and slowly swept the porch. Then I watered Sarah's plants. Caleb cleaned out the wood stove and carried the ashes to the barn, spilling them so that I had to sweep the porch again.

"I *am* loud and pesky," Caleb cried suddenly. "You said so! And she has gone to buy a train ticket to go away!"

"No, Caleb. She would tell us."

"The house is too small," said Caleb. "That's what it is."

"The house is not too small," I said.

I looked at Sarah's drawing of the fields pinned up on the wall next to the window.

"What is missing?" I asked Caleb. "You said you knew what was missing."

"Colors," said Caleb wearily. "The colors of the sea."

Outside, clouds moved into the sky and

went away again. We took lunch to Papa, cheese and bread and lemonade. Caleb nudged me.

"Ask him. Ask Papa."

"What has Sarah gone to do?" I asked.

"I don't know," said Papa. He squinted at me. Then he sighed and put one hand on Caleb's head, one on mine. "Sarah is Sarah. She does things her way, you know."

"I know," said Caleb very softly.

Papa picked up his shovel and put on his hat.

"Ask if she's coming back," whispered Caleb.

"Of course she's coming back," I said. "Seal is here." But I would not ask the question. I was afraid to hear the answer.

We fed the sheep, and I set the table for dinner. Four plates. The sun dropped low over the west fields. Lottie and Nick stood at the door, wagging their tails, asking for supper.

Papa came to light the stove. And then it was dusk. Soon it would be dark. Caleb sat on the porch steps, turning his moon snail shell over and over in his hand. Seal brushed back and forth against him.

Suddenly Lottie began to bark, and Nick jumped off the porch and ran down the road.

"Dust!" cried Caleb. He climbed the porch and stood on the roof. "Dust, and a yellow bonnet!"

Slowly the wagon came around the windmill and the barn and the windbreak and into the yard, the dogs jumping happily beside it.

"Hush, dogs," said Sarah. And Nick leaped up into the wagon to sit by Sarah.

Papa took the reins and Sarah climbed down from the wagon.

Caleb burst into tears.

"Seal was very worried!" he cried.

Sarah put her arms around him, and he

wailed into her dress. "And the house is too small, we thought! And I am loud and pesky!"

Sarah looked at Papa and me over Caleb's head.

"We thought you might be thinking of leaving us," I told her. "Because you miss the sea."

Sarah smiled.

"No," she said. "I will always miss my old home, but the truth of it is I would miss you more."

Papa smiled at Sarah, then he bent quickly to unhitch the horses from the wagon. He led them to the barn for water.

Sarah handed me a package.

"For Anna," she said. "And Caleb. For all of us."

The package was small, wrapped in brown paper with a rubber band around it. Very carefully I unwrapped it, Caleb peering closely. Inside were three colored pencils.

"Blue," said Caleb slowly, "and gray. And green."

Sarah nodded.

Suddenly Caleb grinned.

"Papa," he called. "Papa, come quickly! Sarah has brought the sea!"

We eat our night meal by candlelight, the four of us. Sarah has brought candles from town. And nasturtium seeds for her garden, and a book of songs to teach us. It is late, and Caleb is nearly sleeping by his plate and Sarah is smiling at my father. Soon there will be a wedding. Papa says that when the preacher asks if he will have Sarah for his wife, he will answer, "Ayuh."

Autumn will come, then winter, cold with a wind that blows like the wind off the sea in Maine. There will be nests of curls to look for, and dried flowers all winter long. When there are storms, Papa will stretch a rope from the door to the barn so we will not be lost when we feed the sheep and the cows and Jack and Old Bess. And Sarah's chickens, if they aren't living in the house. There will be Sarah's sea, blue and gray and green, hanging on the wall. And songs, old ones and new. And Seal with yellow eyes. And there will be Sarah, plain and tall.

Turn the page for excerpts from the three
other books by Patricia MacLachlan
that follow *Sarah, Plain and Tall*:

Skylark
Caleb's Story
More Perfect than the Moon

From *Skylark*

Papa married Sarah on a summer day. There were no clouds in the sky, and Papa picked Sarah up in his arms and whirled her around and around, her white dress and veil surrounding them like the summer wind. Caleb was so excited and happy, he burst into tears.

Everybody was happy.

1

"Stand on that stump, Caleb. Anna, you next to him. That will be a good family picture."

Joshua, the photographer, looked through his big camera at us as we stood on the porch squinting in the sunlight. Caleb wore a white shirt, his hair combed slick to his head, Sarah in a white dress, Papa looking hot and uneasy in his suit. The lace at my neck itched in the summer heat. We had to be still for so long that Caleb began to whistle softly, making Sarah smile.

Far off in the distance the dogs, Nick and Lottie, walked slowly through the dry prairie grass. They walked past the cow pond nearly empty of water, past the wagon, past the chickens in the yard. Nick saw us first, then Lottie, and they began to run. Caleb looked sideways at me as they jumped the fence and ran to us, running up to stand between Sarah and Papa as if they wanted to be in the picture, too. We tried not to laugh, but Sarah couldn't help it. She looked up at Papa and he smiled down at her. And Joshua took the picture of us all laughing, Papa smiling at Sarah.

Joshua laughed, too.

"Your aunts will like that picture," he said to Sarah.

Sarah fanned herself.

"They hardly know what I look like anymore," she said softly. "I hardly know what *they* look like anymore."

I looked at Caleb. I knew Caleb didn't like to think about Sarah and her aunts and her brother and the sea she had left behind.

"It's Maine you came from, isn't it?" said Joshua.

"Yes," said Sarah.

"She lives *here* now," said Caleb loudly.

Papa put his hand on Caleb's head.

"That she does," said Joshua, smiling.

He turned and looked out over the cornfield, the plants so dry they rattled in the wind.

"But I bet Maine is green," Joshua said in a low voice. He looked out over the land with a faraway look, as if he were somewhere else. "We sure could use rain. I remember a long time ago, you remember it, Jacob. The water dried up, the fields so dry that the leaves fell like dust. And then the winds came. My grandfather packed up his family and left."

"Did he come back?" asked Caleb.

Joshua turned.

"No," he said, "he never came back."

Joshua packed up the last of his things and got up in his wagon.

Papa looked at Sarah.

"It will rain," he said.

We watched the wagon go off down the road.

"It will rain," Papa repeated softly.

From Caleb's Story

Anna has done something terrible. She has given me a journal to fill.

She wants me to write about the farm while she's gone, finishing school, working in town.

In Anna's journal the words walk across the page like bird prints in the mud. But it is hard for me. It is hard to find things to write about. Not much happens here, I told Anna. Chores, schoolwork, and more chores. Anna tells me I'll find something to write. Things to write about are all around you, she says.

I don't think so. There's only the cold, the skies as gray as goose feathers. And the wind.

Always the wind.

—Caleb Witting

1

"Come find me, Caleb!" called my little sister, Cassie.

She ran out the door and down the steps. Lottie barked and followed her. Nick was older than Lottie. He stayed on the porch and watched.

"I don't have time. I mean it, Cassie!"

Cassie ignored me the way she always did when she wanted something.

"And don't look!" she called.

I sighed and walked after her. I covered my eyes with my hand, but through my fingers I could see Cassie run to the barn.

"One, two, three," I counted.

"Slower," she cried.

"Four . . . five . . . five and a half."

Papa was hitching Bess to the wagon.

"Don't be long," he said. "Anna's almost ready to leave."

"Don't worry. This won't take long, Papa."

"I don't know, Caleb. Cassie's getting better at hiding."

I laughed.

"At least you don't see her feet sticking out anymore. Six, seven, eight, nine, ten," I called.

I could hear Cassie laughing, but I couldn't see her. I walked into the barn. It was cool and dark and quiet. A winter sharp smell filled the space.

"Cassie?"

There was no answer. There was a time when Cassie would answer me and give away her hiding place—she couldn't help it. Not today.

May, my favorite of all our horses, was in her stall. I reached over and touched her nose, and she nickered at me. I could see her breath in the cold air. There was silence, the only sound the sound of May's breathing. Then I heard Lottie's bark outside, and Cassie's voice.

"Cassie? I hear you!"

I turned. Cassie tried to run by the barn door, and I rushed out and caught her, making her squeal.

"I've got you, Pal!"

Cassie laughed and we began to walk back to the house, Lottie leaping and jumping in front of us. Cassie reached up and took my hand, her face suddenly serious.

"There's a man."

"What man?"

"Behind the barn," said Cassie. "He's wrapped in a green blanket. He asked me about Papa."

I smiled.

"You and your imaginary friends, Cassie."

She scowled at me.

"There's a man," she insisted.

"You're stubborn," I told her. "Like Sarah."

"Like Mama," Cassie corrected me. "You could call her Mama."

"I could," I said. "But you know the story, Cassie. When she first came here Anna and I called her Sarah. We will always call her Sarah."

"I will call her Mama," said Cassie.

I picked her up—she was so light—and Cassie put her head on my shoulder as we walked to the house.

"A man," she whispered in my ear.

Hello. I am writing here now. My brother Caleb says it is my turn to keep the journal. He is busy working the farm most of the time, and when haying time comes he'll be busy all the time.

I am almost in third grade. I can spell, you know. And I know many words, some of them important words. Like

windswept

imagination

ecstatic.

I will have to look up the meaning of ecstatic. But I can spell it.

I am a watcher. I am a listener, too. I am invisible. I can make myself so small and quiet and hidden that sometimes no one knows

I am there to watch and listen.

Except for Grandfather. He finds me everywhere. He sees me when I'm hiding. Grandfather
tells me he can see through walls.

But he won't stop me.

I will find lots to write about.

Watch me.

—Cassandra Sarah Witting

1

Summer was cool and wet, and the barn-yard was muddy. It was like spring left over. The cats jumped from the fence and ran into the barn so they could sleep in the dry hay.

"I see you there, you know," Grandfather called to me. "Hiding behind Martha."

Grandfather knew the names of all our cows. Martha was black, with a white spot on her rump.

I stood up.

"I'm not hiding," I said. "I'm studying Martha's spot."

This made Grandfather smile. And Caleb.

"You were hiding," said Grandfather. "It made Martha nervous. I could see her eyes roll."

Martha turned and stared at me.

"Martha always rolls her eyes," I told Grandfather.

He laughed out loud. He and Caleb were digging trenches in the mud so the rains would run off.

"You're sneaky, Cassie," said Caleb.

"Elusive," I told him. "Mama says I'm elusive."

"Sarah always finds a word to make you look better," said Caleb. "I say you're sneaky."

Caleb has always called Mama Sarah. My mama is not Caleb's real mama. But she is mine. He and Anna called her Sarah when she first came to meet Papa. Before they were married. I call her Mama. Maybe someday I'll call her Sarah.

"I'm looking for things to write about," I told Caleb. "It just looks like I'm sneaky."

I took my notebook out of my coat pocket and began reading to them.

" 'Grandfather and Caleb dug deep rivers in the mud so the cows, Martha, Eleni, Princess, Mary Louise, Pudgie, and Boots, can float into the barn to feed.' "

"That's not the truth!" said Caleb.

"Yes it is," I said. "It is storytelling."

"Made up," said Caleb.

"Maybe," I said, turning away and walking through the mud to the barn. I turned once to see Grandfather smiling at me, Caleb staring.

"Maybe," I said louder just before I disappeared into the dark barn.